DREAMWORKS TROLLHUNTERS
TALES OF ARCADIA
FROM GUILLERMO DEL TORO

Jim Lake Jr.'s
Survival Guide

By Cala Spinner

Simon Spotlight
New York   London   Toronto   Sydney   New Delhi

Handwriting Key:

Jim

Blinky

Claire

Toby

SIMON SPOTLIGHT

An imprint of Simon & Schuster Children's Publishing Division

1230 Avenue of the Americas, New York, New York 10020

This Simon Spotlight hardcover edition December 2017

DreamWorks Trollhunters © 2017 DreamWorks Animation LLC. All Rights Reserved.

All rights reserved, including the right of reproduction in whole or in part in any form.

SIMON SPOTLIGHT and colophon are registered trademarks of Simon & Schuster, Inc.

For information about special discounts for bulk purchases, please contact Simon & Schuster Special Sales at 1-866-506-1949 or business@simonandschuster.com.

Designed by Brittany Naundorff

The text of this book was set in Flunkie Calligraphr.

Manufactured in China 0917 RKT

10 9 8 7 6 5 4 3 2 1

ISBN 978-1-5344-1321-4

ISBN 978-1-5344-1322-1 (eBook)

DO NOT READ THIS JOURNAL! If this journal has somehow fallen into your hands, I repeat, do NOT read it.

I don't care if it's whispering your name. I don't care if it's glowing blue. I'm telling you right now: you're better off not reading any of this.

Why? Because you're better off not knowing about Trolls and Gumm-Gumms and Changelings. You're better off not knowing about Gunmar and Killahead Bridge and the Darklands. And if for some reason my warnings mean nothing and you're still reading this, you're way, waaaaay better off not knowing about what's happening at Arcadia Oaks High.

So, just close this book right now. Trust me, you'll thank yourself later.

Apologies, Master Jim. We read your journal.

Becoming the Trollhunter

If you've stuck around, and I haven't snatched this journal back, something must have happened to me. So, hear me out. I can't promise that you'll like everything you read.

See, my life is pretty weird. It used to be normal, but then I became the Trollhunter.

And nothing has been normal since.

How did I end up becoming the Trollhunter? Here's my story. I guess you could say it all started with meatloaf sandwiches. You see, if I hadn't made meatloaf sandwiches, Toby and I wouldn't have been late for school.

Tobias "Toby" Domzalski

Toby is my best friend. Tobes is always there for me no matter what—unless he's getting his braces adjusted, in which case, he'll be there for me after his orthodontist appointment.

That's right, Jimbo. You can count on me—as long as the metal in my mouth isn't going haywire.

That morning, Toby and I decided to take a shortcut through the canals because we were running late. But then something weird happened. I heard a voice coming from a pile of rocks.

"James Lake," the voice said. (That's my full name. Actually, it's James Lake Jr., but everyone calls me Jim.)

Toby and I crawled over to the rubble. He was convinced there was a walkie-talkie or something around, but there was no walkie-talkie.

There was, however, a glowing blue Amulet.

Just then, the final bell rang for homeroom.

We had to hurry. I grabbed the Amulet and tossed it into my backpack. We took off, speeding over to school as fast as we could.

Thankfully, we didn't get detention. But I did fall asleep in history class. Our teacher Mr. Strickler noticed.

Mr. Strickler thought it would be a good idea to talk to my mom. He also had some extra advice. . . .

"Jim, if you fancy Miss Nuñez, I submit that 'talking to' will be much more effective than 'staring at,'" he said.

I nodded and walked away.

Yikes! Was it that obvious I had a crush on Claire Nuñez?

In gym class I spotted Claire on the bleachers with

Claire is one of the most beautiful girls at Arcadia Oaks High. But she's not just beautiful—she's smart and funny, too, and really likes guacamole. Unfortunately, Claire is always surrounded by her friends, so it's really hard to talk to her alone.

Claire Nuñez

her friends Darci Scott and Mary Wang. I took a step in their direction. My hands felt clammy. I stared right at them. But Mr. Strickler was right. If I wanted to talk to Claire, I had to, you know, talk to Claire.

"Buenas noches," I said finally. Inside, I kicked myself for using the Spanish word for "night."

The girls got up to leave, but Claire stayed behind for a second. Her brown eyes bore right into mine, and somehow, even though I was nervous, she made me feel a little better about myself.

"Do you like Shakespeare?" Claire asked.

"What?" I asked. Was Claire really talking to me?!

"The school play," she explained, handing a flyer to me. "We're having trouble getting boys to audition."

Then she walked away.

And she smiled at me.

This is REAL LIFE!!! Claire Nuñez smiled at me!

You know, I thought, *maybe I owe Mr. Strickler a thank-you or two.*

After gym class, I told Toby all about my conversation with Claire.

"You should totally do the play," Toby said. "You're always saying how you want your life to be more exciting, right?"

"I don't think *Romeo and Juliet* is exactly the answer, Tobes," I responded. "I—I just need to know that there's something more to life than high school."

If I'm being honest, I always wanted to go on an adventure. You know, something that means something. My mom goes on an adventure every day when she helps sick people feel better. She's a doctor. And me, at that point, my biggest adventure was struggling to keep the backyard raccoons out of the trash bins.

In the afternoon, as Toby and I walked by the lockers outside, we ran into Steve Palchuck.

Steve is ... well ... Steve is mean. He's the school bully at Arcadia Oaks High and almost everyone is afraid of him. He's strong and stuffs people into lockers, and likes to solve problems by fighting.

Steve Palchuck

At the moment Steve was stuffing a smaller kid, Eli, into a locker.

Poor Eli, I thought. It just wasn't fair that he was getting picked on. You know how I really wanted an adventure? Well, I guess being adventurous is standing up to the bully. I had to do something. I marched over to Steve.

"Look, Steve," I said. "Just let him out."

Steve seemed surprised that I had approached him. He turned. He stopped picking on Eli, which was good, but then he grabbed me. Which was bad.

"Or you'll do what?" he sneered.

"Okay. Do it. Punch me," I said.

"You're asking for a beating?" He laughed.

I braced myself.

Steve was just about ready to punch me when Coach Lawrence appeared.

Coach Lawrence glanced all around. No one dared say a word. We should have involved the adults since Steve was bullying us, but it just didn't happen that way. Then Coach Lawrence left and Steve followed him to practice. I was safe . . . for now.

I guess I got so busy with the Claire and Steve stuff I forgot about how the day started—with a talking Amulet. But after I said hello to my mom after school, I took the Amulet out of my backpack and studied it. It started to glow.

My mom is the best person I know. Ever since my dad left when I was five, it's just been my mom and me. She's kind and caring. She's also a doctor at Arcadia Oaks Hospital. She does something I only wish I could do: she saves people.

Mom and I promised that we'd take care of each other. I help her with things like cooking, and sometimes I'll even polish her glasses. I don't mind it, though. Besides, I really don't trust Mom to make my famous egg-white Manchego omelet!

My mom: Barbara Lake

Amulet of
← Daylight

"Um, hi,"
I said to the
Amulet a little
sheepishly. "How
are you doing?
I'm Jim. But then,
you knew that,
because you spoke
my name. Which is weird."
If only I could go back in
time and tell myself more . . . like the Amulet I'd found is
actually the Amulet of Daylight, a powerful piece of magic
created by Merlin, the wizard. To activate the Amulet,
you have to say, "For the glory of Merlin, Daylight is mine
to command." But I'd learn all that soon. . . .

Just then, I heard a crash from below. I left the
Amulet behind.

I went down to the basement, ready to investigate . . .
and saw something with six eyes! Six eyes?! And they were
attached to a . . . to a . . . Troll!

"Master Jim!" the Troll said. "I am known as Blinkous
Galadrigal. But you may call me Blinky, if you like."

As if that wasn't terrifying enough, there was another Troll too—this one covered in green moss!

"Hi," this new Troll breathed.

"Aagh!" I screamed.

"It's AAARRRGGHH!!!. Three Rs," the Troll corrected.

"Master Jim!" Blinky exclaimed. "You have been chosen."

Chosen? For what? To be Troll dinner?

"The Amulet of Daylight challenges you to ascend to the most sacred of offices. Means responsibility. Unbeknown to your kind, there is a secret world, a vast civilization of Trolls lurking beneath your feet," Blinky continued.

Amulet of Daylight? Trolls? Secret world? I could barely think.

"And it is now your charge to protect them, for you, Master Jim, are the Trollhunter. This honor is yours to accept."

Trolls. Two Trolls in my house. Something about being a "Trollhunter." The Amulet. This was too much. I started to feel woozy. My vision blurred, and my eyes got foggy, and . . .

I passed out.

Well, you can't say I was impolite. I did introduce myself, after all.

Blinky and AAARRRGGHH!!!

Blinky and AAARRRGGHH!!! are the two Trolls who showed up at my house after the Amulet chose me as Trollhunter.

Ah, Master Jim, I see that you've left our section quite sparse. No matter, I can understand now that we surprised you. I am Blinky, also known as Blinkous Galadrigal, chief Troll adviser. I come to you having trained Trollhunters of eras past, like Unkar the Unfortunate. My counterpart is AAARRRGGHH!!!, formerly known as Aarghaumont. AAARRRGGHH!!! was once a general in the evil Gunmar's army, but later absconded from his flesh-eating ways and became a pacifist. No need to fear us, Master Jim!

The next morning I walked into Mr. Strickler's office and took a seat. Since he had given good advice about Claire, he might in this situation too.

Mr. Strickler

Mr. Strickler is everyone's favorite teacher at Arcadia Oaks High. Although he caught me sleeping in class, he was pretty cool about it. Strickler is calm, smart, and has a lot of cool-looking stuff in his office.

"Last night, two . . . um, things, showed up at my house," I told him. "You know—things! Guys. But really weird. One had these eyes, and the other one was huge and hairy, and they said that they were Tro—"

Suddenly, I realized how crazy this all must sound to Mr. Strickler. Who was I kidding? The only thing this would help with is getting me sent to the school nurse.

"Trainers!" I blurted, trying to fix my mistake.

"Trainers. Who want to train me in . . . chess," I

finished. "They . . . really weirded me out."

"It's like I told you yesterday," said Strickler. "You have a lot on your shoulders. Too much, in my opinion. And I think this opportunity—"

"Chess," I butt in.

"I think it's causing you anxiety. It's as a great poet once wrote, 'Do what's good for you or you're not good for anybody.'"

As usual, Mr. Strickler's advice was on point. I just couldn't be the Trollhunter. I couldn't do it.

I thanked Mr. Strickler and headed out of his office.

After school, I decided to inspect the Amulet again. It had started glowing when I was in Strickler's office, and I couldn't figure out why. Words in a strange language appeared on its edge and then morphed into English.

"For the glory of Merlin, Daylight is mine to command,'" I read. The Amulet glowed brighter and brighter. It gathered me in the light . . . and lifted me six feet into the air. And like magic, the most incredible armor surrounded me!

Trollhunter Armor

As I later learned, the Trollhunter Armor is a sleek set of armor made for the Trollhunter. It takes shape to fit the Trollhunter, which is good because at first my armor was too big, but then it shrunk down to fit me perfectly. It's made out of pure sunlight. Thankfully, this provides additional protection against the evil Trolls, who are resistant to the light. But more on them later. Also worthy of note: the armor reacts to your emotional state. So if you're in distress, it activates. Sometimes when you don't want it to.

And just when I thought things were over, a sword appeared with the armor.

Sword of Daylight

A powerful weapon belonging to the Trollhunter.
The Sword of Daylight is activated when a Trollhunter
incants "For the glory of Merlin, Daylight is mine to command!"

After that I was so excited! This was beyond amazing! The
second Toby was finished with the dentist the next day . . .

"Oh my gosh, oh my gosh, oh my gosh, so cool! Dude!
You know what this means, right? You have a sacred
responsibility here!" Toby screeched. "You have to use
these new powers for the benefit of all mankind!" His eyes
narrowed on me. "You have to use this to kick Steve's butt!"

"Really? I show you a glowing sword and a suit of
armor that can only be magic, and that's how you respond?"
I asked.

Before anything else happened, there was a knock at
the door. It was Blinky.

"Master Jim!" Blinky exclaimed, and bounded into the
room. "You told your little friend about us?" Blinky asked,
eyeing Toby.

"Um, is that a problem?" It's not, you know, like this Trollhunter thing came with a manual or anything.

"Master Jim, we Trolls have gone to great lengths to keep our existence secret from your kind, lest there be panic. The Mantle of Trollhunter is a sacred responsibility, one which has never been passed to a human before. This is a momentous occasion," Blinky explained.

"So the previous Trollhunter, what, retired?" I asked.

"Turned to stone and smashed," Blinky said. "Kanjigar the Courageous was his name. Brutally slain by a ruthless Troll named Bular."

Kanjigar the Courageous

Kanjigar was the Trollhunter before me. He sacrificed himself to keep the Amulet out of the hands of evil. He was brave and valiant, renowned as one of the best warriors in the world. The only problem is, he's dead. So I don't want to follow in his footsteps.

See Bular? Yeah, he's pretty scary. Bular is a Gumm-Gumm Troll, which means he's one of the bad Trolls. What makes a bad Troll, you ask? Well, bad Trolls eat humans. So let's just say we don't want a whole bunch of bad Trolls around. Bular wants to destroy the Trollhunters one by one . . . which means Bular wants to destroy, well, me.

Bular

"Don't worry, dude. This Bular guy probably just got lucky," Toby told me.

"The evidence does not suggest that," Blinky said.

My head was spinning. Was it only two days ago we'd even found the stupid Amulet in the first place?

"The Amulet called to you, Master Jim. It chose you. It is your sacred obligation. You cannot refuse it; you cannot give it back. It is yours until you die. Master Jim, you are now responsible for the protection of two worlds: human and Troll alike. If you do not keep the balance, evil Trolls like Bular will come into yours, the human world, and wreak havoc," said Blinky. "With the Amulet now in your possession, Bular will seek you out, and you will face him, one way or another."

I could feel the blood rush to my head again. Oh no. Was I going to pass out? I couldn't pass out. Not again!

"Maybe what Jim needs is a little time to process all this. You laid a lot of heavy stuff on him," Toby said, seemingly totally okay with all this.

Blinky nodded. "We shall return tomorrow, then! To begin your training."

"Awesome sauce," said Toby.

I stared at the Amulet. Its blue gemstone glistened at me, shining like it was the key to all the world's secrets. I tried to see if there was some way I could take back the incantation and the "Mantle of Trollhunter," like Blinky had put it. But then Blinky started speaking.

"Master Jim, if I may . . . Destiny is a gift. Some go their entire lives living an existence of quiet desperation, never learning the truth that what feels as though a burden is pushing down upon our shoulders is actually the sense of purpose that lifts us to greater heights. Never forget that fear is but the precursor to valor, that to strive and triumph in the face of fear is what it means to be a hero. Don't think, Master Jim. Become."

The next day at school, Toby and I were walking around when a glow started emanating from my backpack. It was the Amulet.

"Oh no," I muttered. I couldn't change into the armor! Not here at school!

Toby, thankfully, is a quick thinker. He shoved me into the gym locker room so the armor could envelop me.

Unfortunately, Mr. Strickler happened to be walking by during this whole ordeal.

"Jim. I don't believe that's appropriate school attire," he said, seeing me.

"It's, uh, for *Romeo and Juliet* tryouts," I said on the spot.

"Hm. Well, you'd better hurry, then," Mr. Strickler said. "I believe auditions end in five minutes."

There was no way out of this one. I'd have to go to the school audition and try out for the play. And embarrass myself in front of Claire.

When it was my turn to audition, I felt like I was going to pass out again, only this time it would be in front of everybody—and Claire. I took a big breath of air.

"Uh," I breathed. Great. Just great. One word in, and I'm already making a fool of myself. "Destiny is a gift. Some go their entire lives living an existence of quiet desperation . . ."

I was using Blinky's speech, but the audience hung on to my every word. Suddenly, I felt a lot more at ease. I stood up straight and tall.

"Never learning the truth that what feels as though a burden is pushing down upon our shoulders is actually the sense of purpose that lifts us to greater heights. Never forget that fear is but the precursor to valor, that to strive and triumph in the face of fear is what it means to be a hero. Don't think. Become."

I took out my sword and showed it to everyone. Everyone stared, then cheered! Everyone—including Claire!

Toby and I rode our bikes home from school, still reeling from my audition. Maybe being the Trollhunter wasn't going to be so bad after all.

Just as I was thinking this, a huge pair of legs lumbered in front of us.

It was a Troll. A big Troll. A big, vicious Troll.

"Trollhunter. Merlin's Creation. Gunmar's Bane," the Troll said, speaking to me. "The Amulet. Surrender it, and I will give you a speedy death."

No doubt about it, this Troll was Bular.

I did the only thing I could think of: I grasped the Amulet and whispered the incantation. But it wasn't working.

Bular lumbered closer.

On our bikes, Toby and I raced as fast as we could away from him. Finally, we ducked behind a store. The gap was so narrow, Bular couldn't make it through.

On the other side of the Stuart Electronics store, Blinky and AAARRRGGHH!!! popped out.

"You have a sweet voice, but you bring death with you!" Toby said, pointing to him.

"Follow me! We'll be safe in Heartstone Trollmarket," Blinky said.

The four of us raced all throughout our town of Arcadia Oaks, trying desperately to avoid being eaten—or worse—by Bular. We darted between trees and through streets.

"Master Jim! Don your armor," Blinky instructed as Bular chased us.

"I've been trying! The Amulet won't listen to me," I told him.

"Did you speak the incantation?" he asked.

"I've been incanting! And it's not working!" I screamed.

"Just focus and incant, dude," Toby said.

But Bular was gaining. He was gaining so fast, he was

about to strike. He did strike. He punched me right in the chest, and— and—THE ARMOR ACTIVATED!

Woo-hoo! Finally! The armor blocked Bular's punch just as he collided with my chest plate. Thankfully, the armor allowed me to leap to safety, but it wasn't over yet.

Meanwhile, Blinky reached into his pocket and pulled out what looked like a small crystal. He tossed it to AAARRRGGHH!!!.

Horngazels

These magical crystal chalks are the keys that open up the portal to Heartstone Trollmarket. To use one, draw a half circle on the wall below the Arcadia Bridge with it, and the portal will open.

Right before Bular was about to deal the killing blow, I was pulled through the wall via Horngazel and into Heartstone Trollmarket.

Heartstone Trollmarket

Heartstone Trollmarket, or just Trollmarket, is a hidden world underneath Arcadia Oaks and home to the Trolls. Trolls live here in peace: they gather together, eat together, and live happily among one another.

Trollmarket is also a safe space for Trolls. Bad Trolls, known as Gumm-Gumms, are forbidden entry.

Heartstone Trollmarket was, in a word, spectacular. Light glowed everywhere. It was unlike anything I'd ever seen—a vast metropolis: half bazaar, half carnival.

"Trollmarket is home and hearth and sanctuary for all good Trolls," Blinky explained.

"Good Trolls?" Toby asked. It was a question I had too. Being the Trollhunter, and friends with Trolls, didn't . . . really . . . make sense.

"Trolls are no different from humans, Tobias. Just as you have the morally compromised in your midst, so do we. The sacred charge of the Trollhunter is to keep the balance," Blinky explained.

Blinky and AAARRRGGHH!!! led us all around Heartstone Trollmarket. We passed shops and different kinds of Trolls. Some wore elaborate jewelry and some had many eyes. A few ate glass bottles happily, like they were pieces of candy.

As we continued walking, we passed a group of Gnomes.

As Blinky and AAARRRGGHH!!! continued to lead us around Heartstone Trollmarket, we ran across another large and intimidating-looking Troll, Draal.

Gnomes

According to Blinky, Gnomes are "vermin." They're pickpockets and scavengers, but the Trolls tolerate them for their grooming services. Gnomes eat the parasites that live on larger Trolls.

"What is this?" Draal thundered. His eyes squared on me. "Who is this fleshbag?"

Blinky, oblivious to whatever Draal was thinking, beamed with pride.

"He is the new Trollhunter," Blinky said.

Draal the Deadly, known as Draal, is the son of Kanjigar. He thought he was the Amulet's rightful heir, so he has it in for me. Draal is a brute with impressive physical power and absolutely no sense of humor.

Draal the Deadly

Tour of the Heartstone Trollmarket

Crystal Stairs: These stairs lead you into the Trollmarket, after you enter with a Horngazel.

Hero's Forge: A massive training arena along the narrow bridge that is home to statues of past Trollhunters. As Blinky explains, these Trollhunter predecessors all come from a line that reaches back to the age of Merlin. This is the final resting place of Kanjigar, the previous Trollhunter. Blinky says one day I will be in this arena too. *But not soon, Jimbo*

The Pit: Part training station, part "find out if you're worthy of the Amulet or not" station. More on that later.

Bagdwella's Fine Gifts: A shop that sells, you guessed it, gifts.

Troll Pub: A place for Trolls to gather. This is their social area, where they can eat, talk, and be merry (though I haven't seen much merriment, if I'm being honest).

RotGut's Apothecary: This is the place to go if you need fine charms, totems, or spells. Sometimes Rot and Gut won't want to give up their merchandise, so it's wise to have a bag of sweaty socks. They can't refuse argyle.

Blinky's Overview of Gumm-Gumms
(That Means Bad Trolls)

It is all recorded in *A Brief Recapitulation of Troll Lore* by the Venerable Bedehilde, but I understand, Master Jim, this is the journal you so desperately wanted to keep as a "manual," as you call it, so I will oblige. Yes, as you wrote, Gumm-Gumms are bad Trolls. In Troll speak, "Gumm-Gumm" means "bringer of horrible, slow, painful, and thoroughly calculated death." The Gumm-Gumms are led by Gunmar, Bular's father, who was banished to the Darklands centuries ago with the rest of them. They seek to escape the Darklands and take over, bringing with them a new era of darkness and desperation.

The Gumm-Gumms are in the Darklands, and they've been trying to infiltrate our world for centuries. Their henchmen dwell among us, and some of their cronies do their bidding in secret.

Just as Blinky was about to start my training, Vendel, an elderly Troll, arrived. Vendel was dubious of the Amulet's decision in choosing me and wanted something called the "Soothscryer" to test me.

I stood in place, and a huge statue came out of the floor. It had dangerously sharp stone teeth arranged in a circle. Vendel instructed that I insert my right hand into its mouth.

Vendel

For the millionth time in the past few days, I gulped. Then I put my hand into the Soothscryer.

The stone teeth whirred and spun all around. The stone clamped down. I was terrified I would lose my arm. Finally, it stopped.

"Inconclusive," Vendel announced. "There's never been a human to bear the mantle before. The Soothscryer needs more time to render its judgment." Then he glared at me. "Let us all hope you live long enough to see it."

Thankfully, Blinky let me off the hook after that— for the night, anyway. I went home, thinking up a cover story for where I'd been.

When I got inside, I spotted my mom sharing a cup of coffee with . . . Mr. Strickler.

"Mr. Strickler came by to congratulate you," Mom said.

"I have to say, Jim, it's a great honor that you've been chosen to wield this mantle. I've no doubt that you'll prove equal to the task," Mr. Strickler said.

Hold up. "Wield this mantle"? Did Mr. Strickler know about me becoming the Trollhunter?

"Jim, surely you knew you'd won the part of Romeo after your breathtaking audition," Mr. Strickler said.

Wait—I got the part? I was going to be Romeo in the school play opposite Claire as Juliet?

"Just be careful, my young Atlas. In Greek mythology Atlas, too, carried the weight of the world on his shoulders," Strickler said.

I'm concerned, I thought. I'm the most concerned! But unless you can figure out a way to make Vendel and Draal and the rest of the Trolls in Heartstone Trollmarket like me, and make Bular stop wanting to kill me, and protect everyone from evil Trolls, there's just nothing I can do about it.

So Much to Learn

So, that's how I ended up as the Trollhunter. I decided that I needed to make my journal into a document of sorts, just in case anything happens to me. A guide, if you will. Which means if you're reading this . . . best of luck.

The next day I joined Blinky for some training in the Hero's Forge. That's where he taught me the three rules of Trollhunting.

The Trollhunter's Rules

Trollhunters live and die by three rules, so I guess you can say they're pretty important.

Rule 1: Always be afraid.

As Blinky says, "Fear is good. keeps us alert. keeps us on guard. makes us vigilant. A hero is not fearless. but someone not stopped by fear."

Rule 2: Always finish the fight.

And by "finish." Trolls mean "kill."

Rule 3: When in doubt. always kick them in the gronk-nuks.

Because apparently. if all else fails. this will do the trick.

"Not the most honorable of tactics. but invariably effective." Blinky says.

As I underwent some training, Draal and Vendel stopped by to see how it was going. Though "see how it was going" is probably an understatement. They stopped by to torment me.

"I thought the great Trollhunter might accept my services as a sparring partner. Part of your training regimen," Draal said with a wicked smile.

Blinky tried to protest, but Vendel was on Draal's side.

"Let them spar," he said.

There was no way out of it. Barely even started training, and I'd have to take on Draal in the Hero's Forge.

"Trust yourself," Blinky said to me.

A sizable crowd of Trolls started to trickle in. Then on Vendel's word, the sparring began.

Have you ever gone up in battle with a massive Troll like Draal? Probably not, so let me tell you, it's not fun. Although I had my armor and sword, Draal sent me flying backward with a single punch.

Draal pinned me down and walked out of the pit.

I was hurt and angry. What was I thinking? What was anyone thinking? An Amulet can't decide someone is a Trollhunter or not. There are Trolls like Draal who have been training their whole lives for this—not some measly fifteen-year-old kid who just so happened to take a shortcut one day. I headed for the exit. I felt ashamed.

Blinky tried to comfort me. "Master Jim, despite whatever doubts you may have about the Amulet's choice, it is now bonded to you. This is a mantle you cannot refuse."

"Watch me," I said.

I left Heartstone Trollmarket and went home. I was so angry that I took out the Amulet and threw it into the garbage. But no matter what I did, the Amulet kept coming back. It followed me.

I guess I was stuck with it. Ugh.

But you know what?! If I was stuck with it, it was time to get serious. I would learn everything I could from Blinky. I'd face Draal again,
and this time I'd win!

A Brief History of Trolls

For centuries the Troll and human worlds stood separate and at peace. But the Gumm-Gumms desired power over all mankind. It didn't help that they also wanted to eat them.

The flesh-eating Trolls were led by Gunmar. The rest of us Trollkind took a stand against him in the shadow of the Killahead Bridge. After many moons of violence and horror, good triumphed over evil.

The Trollhunter locked Gunmar and his forces away by exiling them to the Darklands. Then the Trollhunter sealed the Killahead Bridge with the Amulet, before we tore it apart, stone by stone.

We left the old world in search of peace. We sailed across oceans to a strange and exotic realm called New Jersey. We kept walking until we found a new Heartstone under Arcadia Oaks. It would be our new home.

A couple of days later in Heartstone Trollmarket, Bagdwella screamed. There was a rogue Gnome about, and she wanted me to catch him.

"The Trollhunter cannot refuse the call," Blinky said.

It looked like I was going to have to deal with this Gnome.

Now, listen. I don't know much about Gnome-hunting in the way a regular Trollhunter would do it. But I do know how I'd Gnome-hunt my way, and this is how.

How to Catch a Gnome:
The Jim Lake Jr. Way

Gnomes are tricky creatures. For example, they'll take your Nougat Nummy bar faster than you can say "For the glory of Merlin."

In the event your Gnome happens to take something more valuable—say, the Amulet of Daylight—things become a little more dire.

Maybe it's not the best method, but it's the Jim Lake Jr. method, and for that, I recommend shrinking down to the Gnome's size. There's a machine in Heartstone Trollmarket—the Furgolator—that will shrink you down. Word of warning, though: it's usually used for minerals, not humans. Don't worry, you'll be fine. Ish.

When the Furgolator hatch finally opens, you may find yourself coughing a lot. That is okay because in addition to coughing, you'll be something else: really, really small! Some bystanders may call you "Jim the Teeny-Tiny" (or "Whatever-Your-Name-Is the Teeny-Tiny").

Now that you've been shrunken down, it will be easy to infiltrate the Gnome's home.

Once inside, cozy up to the Gnome. You can say something like, "I like Nougat Nummies too. Mind if I have a bite?"

But Gnomes aren't exactly known for being friendly. So if your Gnome attacks, feel free to fight him or her off with a pencil. But do NOT, under any circumstances, touch the Gnome's hat.

Underneath a Gnome's hat is a gnarly horn. Gnomes don't like feeling exposed, so they might charge at you with brute force.

At this point, since you really need to get the Amulet

back, it is A-OK to recite the incantation. But be warned: your armor might be big. Do not be alarmed. It'll shrink down to size in no time.

Once in your armor, you know what to do. Catching the Gnome is pretty easy for a teeny-tiny Trollhunter. Feel free to bag it in a sack and feel triumphant.

After I'd caught the Gnome, Blinky was very pleased.

"Now you have to take care of him," he said.

"Rule number two," AAARRRGGHH!!! reminded me. Always finish the fight.

For Trolls, this means kill.

I didn't want to think about that. I'm not a Troll, and I'm not a killer. I decided to tackle the more pressing matter at hand.

"What about this shrinking stuff? My Spanish presentation is tomorrow. When does it wear off?" I asked.

Blinky didn't miss a beat.

"Don't worry, Master Jim. Sleep it off. By morning you'll be as good as new. And how you have earned it, Jim the Gnome Slayer!"

It's been a whirlwind couple of days. The next morning, after my Gnome-capturing escapade, I woke up in what seemed like a normal-sized bed . . . but it wasn't a normal-sized bed at all—it was a doll bed at Toby's house!

"Why am I still small?" I asked, panicking.

"Maybe stuff works differently on Trolls than it does on humans," Toby guessed. "We have to call you in sick."

"No! Señor Uhl can sniff out a lie a mile away," I said. But then I got an idea. I could video call in my presentation if Toby helped me set up. Toby would go to school, and I'd do my presentation from his room.

So here's another lesson in Trollhunting:

Nana

Nana is Toby's grandmother. Toby lives with her and her many cats, including her favorite—Mr. Meow Meow PI. Nana is also a big fan of true crime TV. Unfortunately—or fortunately, depending on your situation—Nana isn't the most attentive person in the world. She's blissfully unaware that their Japanese foreign exchange student AAARRRGGHH!!! is not Japanese, a student, or even human. Or, if you're shrunken down to size and living inside a dollhouse in her apartment, she might not notice that, either.

sometimes you need to get a little creative.

The Spanish presentation almost went without a hitch . . . almost. But then Nana came into the room, and the Gnome I had captured escaped his sack. You see, I still hadn't finished the fight. Toby and I took the Gnome to his house until we could figure out what to do with him.

In the event you find yourself in a situation with a not-yet-disposed-of Gnome, feel free to tie it up in a sock with a shoelace. You'll be able to do so and finish your Spanish presentation *con mucho tiempo* (that means "with time"—I think).

But then I started growing back to my normal size, on camera!

Thankfully, Toby shut off my live stream and came home.

During the entire time Toby ventured back, I stared at the Gnome. He just wanted a home—just a place to belong. In the dollhouse he even made friends with a superhero doll. That gave me an idea.

"Blinky said we needed to 'take care of him,' but what if we, like, 'take care of him'?" I suggested to Toby. "I know it's not exactly the second rule of Trollhunting, but for this one, maybe we'll do it our own way. Without the murdering."

Toby got very excited.

"Jim, I already have a name. Gnome Chompsky!"

And so Gnome Chompsky joined our ragtag band of Trollhunters.

That's how to take care of a Gnome, the Jim Lake Jr. way!

Goblins

Did you think Gnomes were the only kind of creature lurking about? Well, I'm sorry to tell you this, but they're not. There's also Goblins.

According to Blinky, Goblins are "ruthless tricksters—petty street vandals who leave a wake of destruction." Actually, many of the traffic issues in Arcadia Oaks are because of Goblins. Who would have guessed?

Goblins crave the pheromone from terror. They are also very vindictive creatures. So if one of them, say, gets run over by a delivery truck, they hold a grudge.

The Goblin chant for vengeance is "Waka chaka!" In English it means "He shall be avenged!"

One day Blinky and Toby noticed that a delivery truck driver had driven over a Goblin. He missed the delivery, though, and would be returning at eight.

"I'm not going to let some poor guy become Goblin chow on my watch," I vowed. It was time to put some of my Trollhunting skills to the test.

That night Toby and I went on a stakeout. When the delivery truck driver finally arrived, the Goblins did too. It wasn't just one or two Goblins, though—there were hundreds, with glowing green eyes.

"Stay down and don't make a sound," Blinky instructed. "In their frenzied state they'll attack anything in their path."

We watched as the delivery was made. Eli, the small boy from Arcadia Oaks High, stepped out.

"That's Eli. He's in my class," I told Blinky.

"He was in your class," said Blinky.

The Goblins swarmed around the delivery truck, chanting "Waka chaka! Waka chaka!" They took it over. Like a group of piranhas taking down a whale—if you've ever seen a group of piranhas taking down a whale. Finally, one Goblin stood on top of the truck.

"Chaka-wa!" the Goblin screeched. (Which, if you don't speak Goblin, is translated into "He is avenged!")

Thankfully, even though Goblins are vindictive, they don't totally understand the human world. If a truck runs over one of their own, their vengeance is with the truck, not the driver. For now.

Unfortunately, the Goblins were still on the loose. They took Toby's pedometer, which tracked how many steps he walked. And since they took his pedometer, we were able to track them. We tracked them all the way to the museum, which was infested with Goblins.

Inside the museum was also Ms. Nomura, the museum curator. We had to rescue her. But then we realized something BIG.

Ms. Nomura wasn't a regular person. Ms. Nomura was a Troll! A half-human kind of Troll.

"I knew I detected the stink of teenage flesh," Ms. Nomura said when she saw us. Her eyes squared on me. "But a human Trollhunter. That I have never tasted."

"Then let's see how you like the taste of Daylight!" I yelled.

Changelings

Ms. Nomura

Ms. Nomura, as I'd later learn, was a Changeling—an evil Troll that does the bidding of the Gumm-Gumms. Once, Changelings were regular Trolls, but the Gumm-Gumms did nasty business to them, causing them to become Changelings. Changelings are swapped out with human babies. The babies are small enough to slip through the cracks of the Killahead Bridge barrier that keeps the other Gumm-Gumms in the Darklands. (Goblins can also pass through the cracks of Killahead Bridge, making the exchange possible.) Changelings take the form of their familiars, the human children they swap places with, and that child is sent to live in the Darklands. Because Changelings grow up in the sun, they are immune to daylight. Since Changelings are basically part human and part Troll, another word for them is "impure," though it isn't all that kind.

Ms. Nomura and I engaged in a difficult battle. She wielded two large sabers and attempted to mince me. I was able to block her, but honestly, that was pure luck. If you get locked in a war with Ms. Nomura and her sabers, I have no advice for you. Sorry.

Ms. Nomura was about to deliver a blow when I looked around. Something Blinky had said to me in our training session from earlier stuck. Arrogance gets you killed. Well, she was definitely arrogant. I yanked the rug underneath Ms. Nomura. She fell backward and smashed a Goblin.

Ms. Nomura sat up to find the slimy remains of the Goblin underneath her bottom.

Remember when I said Goblins are all about vengeance? Well, thankfully, they weren't vengeful against me for throwing Ms. Nomura into the Goblin's path.

The Goblins leaped up and started attacking Ms. Nomura!

"Let's get outta here!" I yelled at Toby.

Blinky and AAARRRGGHH!!! would take care of the rest. Guess we weren't rescuing Ms. Nomura after all.

Although I was still making mistakes, I felt like I was getting used to the Trollhunter "mantle," as Blinky called it, and decided to challenge Draal to a rematch. But later I learned something terrifying: challenging a Troll's honor, as I did, meant a fight to the death. Which meant Draal was totally going to kill me.

What to Do When You Want to Tell Your Mom You're the Trollhunter Because You Might Die Tomorrow

Unfortunately, there's no perfect way to come out and tell your mom you're the Trollhunter. And there's no perfect way to come out and tell her that you're about to battle the son of the previous Trollhunter.

So instead, cook. Bake all your mom's favorites. Have a nice last meal together. Tell her she's an amazing woman and that you'd never leave her willingly.

Hopefully, she'll remember you fondly.

Barbara Lake's Favorite Foods

Shrimp cakes
Cookies
Blueberry waffles
Bacon mac and cheese

Oh, and another thing: write letters. Here's a letter
I wrote for Claire, just in case.

Dear Claire,

    I know this may sound strange, but
if you're reading this, I have something
important to tell you. I'm a **Trollhunter**. I
have to battle monsters and make sure none
of them escape into our world.

    You're a wonderful girl, Claire. You're
funny and smart and nice. I wish I could be
at play rehearsal more. It's not because I
don't want to be in *Romeo and Juliet*. Trust
me, I do. I want nothing more than to be
there, but I have a sacred obligation. I
just want you to know all that. I hope you
can understand.

                —Jim Lake Jr.

Battling Another Troll: Draal Style

I arrived in the battle arena feeling, well, very rule 1: afraid. Then I put on my Trollhunter armor. And the battle began.

The battle arena's floor moves, so sometimes you're not sure if a step will be a good one or if it will kill you. Draal, on the other hand, curled up into a deadly ball and rolled around menacingly.

I swung my sword, but Draal snatched it out of my hands, and I was left vulnerable and unarmed. Meanwhile, I could hear Blinky's commentary from the sidelines.

"Ten whole seconds! He's not dead. That's a fortuitous sign," Blinky cheered.

Twelve seconds into battle, Draal had me cornered. He leaped up, teeth bared, and delivered a strike. Then he tossed me around like a play toy. My stomach hurt. "Raaaah!" Draal screeched. I was done for, I knew it.

I was on the ground, and Draal approached me. At this point, I had no idea what to do. But I did know that I was very, very afraid.

I used Draal's blind spot to sneak up on him. Then I set him up right in the line of a giant pendulum ax. He was so disoriented, the blade caught him and pummeled him backward. Draal landed near the edge of the moving ground, struggling to hold on.

I raised my sword to Draal's face, but if I hurt him, I'd be no better than the bullies at Arcadia Oaks High. Killing might have been the Troll way, but it certainly wasn't the Jim Lake Jr. way.

I stuck my sword into the ground, claiming victory. Then I reached out a hand to help Draal up.

"Come on, man. Don't make it weird," I told him.

Draal got up, but he was ashamed. The entire Troll crowd started booing him.

Look, I may not have followed the Troll rules, but neither did the Amulet when it chose me.

What Happens After You Don't Finish the Fight

Remember when I said Goblins are vengeful creatures? Well, Trolls are prideful ones. Because I defeated Draal and didn't kill him, he could never show his face in Heartstone Trollmarket again. So Draal moved into my basement and became my protector of sorts, and trainer.

"When the time comes, I will be proud to fight by your side," Draal said.

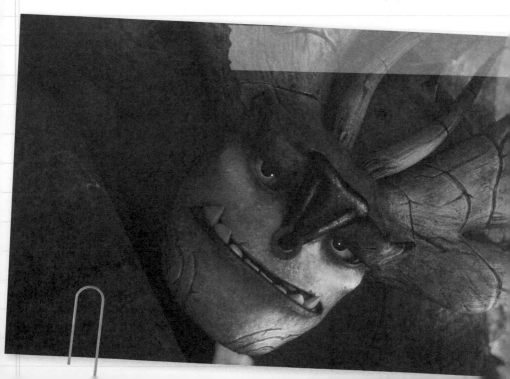

A Brief History of Trollhunters

A long, long time ago, a great wizard and protector by the name of Merlin watched over the Trolls. Merlin created a special Amulet, the Amulet of Daylight, to choose new Trollhunters.

Known former Trollhunters include:

Kanjigar the Courageous

My predecessor. His son is Draal, who would eventually protect me. Kanjigar was fierce and brave, and ultimately sacrificed himself so the Amulet would not fall into Bular's hands.

Unkar didn't last very long in battle—like less than a day—but he's worthy of note because Blinky trained him, too.

Unkar the Unfortunate

Deya the Deliverer

Deya was the Trollhunter who trapped Gunmar and the Gumm-Gumm army in the Darklands by constructing a bridge called Killahead Bridge. She then led the Trolls to the New World and helped build Heartstone Trollmarket.

Killahead Bridge

Killahead Bridge was constructed to trap the Gumm-Gumms in the Darklands. It was then destroyed, and the pieces were scattered so as to seal the Darklands forever.

However, at the museum, Toby took a quick photograph of something Ms. Nomura and the Goblins were trying to put together. It was Killahead Bridge! We learned the bad guys wanted to open the bridge and release Gunmar—which meant there were other Changelings on the loose. I had to catch them and destroy the bridge before it was too late. But when we went back to museum, the pieces were gone. We had to find them!

Gaggletack

Gaggletacks are special horseshoe-shaped objects made of pure iron that can tell you if someone is a Changeling. If a Changeling grasps it, they immediately change into their Troll form.

Toby was convinced his dentist was a Changeling, so he took a Gaggletack to his next appointment. It turned out that Toby's dentist was just a human being (but a merciless one). His assistant, on the other hand . . .

Babysitting a Potential Changeling

One day Toby and I saw a Goblin carrying a baby. The baby dropped a stuffed bunny. We found out later that that stuffed bunny, called Suzy Snooze, belonged to Claire's younger brother, Enrique. Had Claire's brother and a Changeling been swapped?

Of course, of all people to be switched for a Changeling, it had to be Claire's brother! I volunteered to watch Enrique while Claire went to a Papa Skull concert with Steve. If Enrique really had been swapped with a Changeling, I'd figure it out.

While Toby held up the baby, I used the Gaggletack on him. Zap! Enrique turned into a terrible, tiny Troll.

"Stupid flesh-thing," the Changeling hissed. Then he bounded out of Claire's room, causing a huge mess. He even tried to eat Claire's cat.

The Changeling, whom we dubbed "NotEnrique," started chucking food at Toby and me. He was doing everything in his power to create as much of a mess as he possibly could. While NotEnrique blasted music on the stereo, Claire called. Her parents were coming back early, and I'd have to scram.

Let's just say, things did not end well. Claire's parents got home early and were horrified to find me—and all the mess.

I may never be allowed to speak to Claire again, but babysitting did do one thing: it confirmed something important.

Claire's brother was a Changeling, and the Changelings were coming in full force to reconstruct Killahead Bridge.

Stalklings

Stalklings are a special kind of evil flying Troll bird. Unlike other Trolls, Stalklings are immune to sunlight. Unfortunately, not much else is known about them because no one (else) has seen a Stalkling and lived to tell the tale.

On my sixteenth birthday a Stalkling chose me as its prey, which meant it would do everything in its power to kill me. Blinky and AAARRRGGHH!!! said that as long as I was never alone, it wouldn't harm me . . . but it's pretty impossible to never be alone. After play rehearsal, alone is just what happened.

　　The Stalkling found me outside of school. It grabbed me by the foot and thrashed me around.

　　Toby and AAARRRGGHH!!! came out as fast as they could, but I was already in the Stalkling's clutches.

"He's up there! How do we get up there?" I heard Toby say.

"No wings," replied AAARRRGGHH!!!.

Lightning flashed all around as the Stalkling threw me back and forth, toying with me.

Desperate, I wielded my sword. "If I go, we go," I announced.

The sword caught lightning and electrocuted both the Stalkling and me. The Stalkling was so disturbed by being shocked, it dropped me, and I free-fell down to the earth below.

"Hurry! Hurry!" Toby called. AAARRRGGHH!!! raced up ahead and caught me. The Stalkling fell to the ground and crashed into a million pieces.

Another score for the Trollhunter.

Grit-Shaka

Draal and I were training outside my house when I told
him I was nervous about kissing Claire at rehearsal.
Okay, Draal was probably not the best person—er,
Troll—to ask for advice, but I was desperate!

"You are afraid," Draal observed.

"I know, I know, that's the first rule—always be
afraid," I said. "But that's with Trolls, not girls. Girls
are, like, the opposite of Trolls."

Draal thought about that. "If these girls require you

not to be afraid, then you need a Grit-Shaka."

"Is that a protein shake?" I asked.

Draal explained that a Grit-Shaka is a Totem used by the Gumm-Gumms. Wearing a Grit-Shaka banishes all cowardice. Draal gave me a Grit-Shaka, and I wore it around my neck. It made me feel cool, really cool. It made me feel . . . crispy. While wearing the Grit-Shaka, I wasn't afraid of anything, including going into the teachers' lounge to have some of their coffee and taking over the PA system to sing. (Okay, so the Grit-Shaka? Not recommended. It kind of makes you superembarrassing to be around.)

One of the most dangerous things the Grit-Shaka encouraged me to do, however, was challenge Bular. I only survived because of Toby's quick thinking. But facing Bular did give me a fascinating piece of information. He called me Young Atlas.

Grit-Shaka

Young Atlas? My eyes flashed. Over and over again Mr. Strickler had called me "Young Atlas."

And if Bular knew that . . . Strickler must know him. Was Strickler a Changeling?

After meeting at a student-teacher conference, my mom and Strickler kind of hit it off. The next day Strickler came over to my house for dinner.

During dinner, my mom got a phone call and had to step away from the table. When we were alone, Strickler glared at me.

"Bular called you 'Young Atlas' to force this very moment. He told me if I can't get you to hand over the Amulet, I should kill you," said Strickler.

"You would kill me in front of my mom?" I asked. "How about you tell me where the bridge is, and I'll leave your head attached to your body?"

"Enough!" Strickler barked when I'd pummeled him to the ground. He transformed into his Troll form—a tall,

disgusting green Troll with a cape.

"Give me the Amulet," Strickler commanded.

"Come and take it," I hissed. I changed now too—into my Trollhunter armor.

Strickler and I faced off. Unlike when I fought Draal or Bular, however, neither of us wanted to kill the other. He wanted my Amulet, and I wanted to know about the location of Killahead Bridge.

After I dropped my Amulet and picked it up and continued fighting, we had to stop because my mom came back. Whatever battle Strickler and I were engaged in had to end.

"It'll be a shame when I won't have you for a teacher anymore," I told Strickler as he left my house.

While Strickler had dinner with my mom and me, Toby, AAARRRGGHH!!!, NotEnrique, and Blinky infiltrated Strickler's office at school. There, they found *The Book of Ga-huel*, which tells Gumm-Gumm history, and an Antramonstrum.

An Antramonstrum is a smoke monster. It is very dangerous, and is dormant until provoked. That night, they released the Antramonstrum and had to get away from it with pure luck (and some rope-climbing skills, on Toby's part!).

Antramonstrum

Fetch

Also while in Strickler's office, my friends found a Fetch. A Fetch is a portal to the Darklands. It's how Changelings come through. Toby stuck his head into the Fetch and saw into the Darklands. **I never want to see the Darklands again!**

You might be wondering what happened to Claire. See, Claire got my letter, and she kind of hated me because of what happened when I babysat her Changeling brother, and she kind of hated me for missing so much play rehearsal, but things got dangerous when NotEnrique pinned an error on her. I knew Goblins would come for their vengeance soon enough, so I had to rescue her. I snuck into Claire's house. Then I explained everything.

I took a deep breath.

"Okay, how do I say this?" I said. "Your brother has been switched with a Changeling, but now Goblins are after you because of something he did, and now I'm here to save you."

"I always suspected there was something different about you. And now I know. You're crazy," Claire said.

Okay, I'll have to give her that one.

"I can prove it to you!" I said, pulling out the Amulet. Of course, my armor didn't envelop me like it should. Claire tried to kick me out, but then I heard them—the Goblins.

I grabbed Claire's hand, and we raced toward the woods. The Goblins were gaining on us.

"Waka chaka . . . ," the Goblins moaned.

Claire paused. "Those aren't raccoons," she said.

Since my Trollhunter armor wasn't, you know, summoning, I grabbed a bat and fended off as many Goblins as possible. But when two Goblins grabbed me, Claire started throwing debris at them, rescuing me.

I smiled. We'd rescued each other.

The Amulet, as it turns out, was a fake that Strickler had planted. But remember how not too long ago I'd tried getting rid of my real Amulet? It kept coming back to me. Same concept—every time I summoned my armor, the Amulet tried to find me, until finally, it flew out of Strickler's and Bular's clutches and into my hand. I was able to summon the armor and take down these Goblins—for good.

"I should have believed you. Why does something that makes no sense make so much sense now?" Claire asked. Then she sighed, and I could see sadness—real sadness—in her eyes.

"Am I ever going to see my baby brother again?" Claire asked.

"It's . . . complicated," I found myself saying. But I wished that I could do more.

And then I did something that no other

Trollhunter has done before.

I promised Claire one thing: I'd get her brother back from the Darklands, no matter the cost.

Not long after, I got a message from Strickler. He'd captured Blinky. He told me that if I ever wanted to save Blinky, I'd have to go with him to Killahead Bridge. I was pretty sure it was a trap, but so many of my friends had gotten hurt since I became the Trollhunter. I wasn't going to let Blinky get hurt too.

Before heading out I met up with Draal.

"If anything goes wrong, if it means anything, I hope you're the next Trollhunter," I said to him.

"And I hope it won't come to that," said Draal.

I met Strickler in an alleyway, and he led me to Killahead Bridge . . . and Blinky. The bridge had been hidden in the museum this whole time! That's where I learned that Strickler needed the Trollhunter to activate it and free Gunmar and the Gumm-Gumms.

"No, Master Jim! Don't do this! If you release Gunmar and his Gumm-Gumm army, you will be unleashing darkness! The world will not survive Gunmar's reign. One Troll's life is hardly worth putting everyone at risk. Think about Heartstone Trollmarket! Your friends! Your own mother! I trained you better than this," Blinky wailed. I was about to place the Amulet on the bridge when my tracking device started going off.

"He's wearing a tracking device!" shouted Ms. Nomura

from the midst. "You said the Trollhunter was alone."

I smiled. "Not Trollhunter. *Trollhunters*," I corrected. Out came Toby, AAARRRGGHH!!!, and Draal. ←

Listen, Kanjigar may have been a great Trollhunter and all, but he didn't have friends. And that's going to be my difference.

"For the glory of Merlin, Daylight is mine to command!" I incanted. Then we all began our attack.

It was a fearsome fight. We swiped and lunged at the Changelings. We did everything we could. At one point, Strickler forced the Amulet onto the bridge, nearly opening the portal to the Darklands. But then Draal ripped out the Amulet, and the bridge fell to pieces.

After that, Bular came at me with a vengeance. We had traveled all the way to Arcadia Bridge. I used my sword against him. Bular picked me up.

"The Amulet should have never chosen a human,"

Bular said as he hoisted me up. "You're too soft. Easy to kill."

Then I remembered something. You know how Blinky said arrogance leads to death? Well, Bular certainly was being arrogant. And me? I was afraid.

I squeezed out of Bular's clutches and dropped to the ground. From there, I picked up my sword—and plunged it right into Bular's heart.

Bular screamed as the daylight ripped through his body. His head twisted back. And then he dropped into the water below the bridge, dead.

I took a deep breath. I'd killed Bular, son of Gunmar.

And I had just enough time to return to school to play Romeo for opening night of the play!

Being the Trollhunter

So, that's the story of how I became the Trollhunter and defeated Bular. And I've learned so much more since then. Here's everything I learned as the Trollhunter, and everything you'll need to know, too.

Good Luck! (You'll Need It.)

Now that Claire knew about Trolls, she came with us to Heartstone Trollmarket.

"It's . . . it's beautiful," Claire said. She grabbed my hand and ran down the crystal staircase. "I want to live down here!" she exclaimed.

Then Claire met Vendel.

"I am so humbled that you accepted me, the first human female in Heartstone Trollmarket," Claire said, extending her hand in friendship.

"No!" Vendel roared. "I accepted a human Trollhunter and allowed the other one to stay for moral support. But this? A third? It's an infestation!"

Claire smiled. She bowed. And then she started . . . speaking Troll. She explained that NotEnrique had been tutoring her.

Vendel's entire expression changed. "She speaks Troll," he said in disbelief. It seemed that Vendel could accept Claire after all.

What Claire wanted to see most of all, however, was Killahead Bridge. She missed her brother dearly. We took her to where we put it after defeating Bular.

"Hey, buddy. It's your sis. Don't you think I've forgotten about you. We're going to get you back, I promise. See you soon, little *chicharrón*," Claire said into it.

Blinky pulled me aside. He said that if I was going to rescue Enrique, he and AAARRRGGHH!!! were on my side. "For folly or fraught, we are a team," said Blinky.

Unfortunately, at Arcadia Oaks High, I wasn't part of a team. Something worse than you could possibly imagine happened . . . I was nominated for Spring Fling King.

"Our nominees will compete in a series of challenges to win your vote," Coach Lawrence announced.

Oh great, just great, I thought. *How am I going to find time to run for Spring Fling King?*

Ghost Forge: Council of Elder Trollhunters

There may come a time, as the Trollhunter, when the Ghost Forge calls to you. The Ghost Forge, also known as the Void, is a place where the spirits of the previous Trollhunters dwell.

When I first visited the Ghost Forge, Kanjigar and the other Trollhunters chastised me.

They didn't like that I worked with my friends and was planning to take them with me when we went to the Darklands to rescue Enrique.

"Look, I'm not perfect," I told them. "But maybe my friends are the reason I'm the only one here still breathing?"

Despite feeling belittled, you can also train in the Ghost Forge with the Trollhunters of past. This is extremely helpful, but you'll need some thick skin to deal with their comments.

And, I guess, if anything has happened to me, I'll be there too, so say hi.

Triumbric Stones

Bodus's *Final Testament* refers to the Triumbric Stones, "Three forces elemental thou must seek." Together, these stones can create a force strong enough to kill Gunmar.

The Triumbric Stones represent Gunmar's life force. The first

stone is the **Birthstone**, representing, as one might guess, Gunmar's humble beginnings. This stone is a piece of the Heartstone that Gunmar was born from. We uncovered it from Gatto's Keep. The Birthstone can be placed inside the Amulet of Daylight to, in a sense, increase its power. By locking the Birthstone into the Amulet, the Trollhunter is able to summon two Glaives at will. These Glaives interlock to form a sharp-edged boomerang.

The next stone is the **Killstone**, which is the remaining piece of the stone used in Gunmar's first kill. Gunmar killed the Wumpa King. This stone was uncovered in the swamps of the Quagawumps, which is known in the human world as Florida. When situated within the Amulet, the Killstone creates a large warrior's shield.

Lastly, but certainly not least-ly, is the **Eye of Gunmar**. This stone is particularly fascinating because it's Gunmar's eye. Gunmar lost his eye when he found and killed Orlag, the Gumm-Gumm warlord. Once placed within the Amulet, it upgrades the Trollhunter's armor and sword into the Eclipse Armor and Sword of Eclipse.

Final Testament of Bodus: Key Facts and Incantation

According to legend there was a scholar named Bodus who managed to figure out how to wound Gunmar. If we were going to go into the Darklands, I had to learn everything I could about hurting Gunmar. Bodus recorded it all in his book, *The Final Testament of Bodus*. Bodus hid the secret within the book—a message. The message says this:

"In darkest tide when Daylight darest wane,
The Myrddin Wylt*obscured a Shadow's bane.
Three forces Elemental thou must seek,
In marshland, caverns deep, and mountain's peak.
Where worthy perish, ye'll prevail in night,
And Eclipse all who quarry with thy might."

* This is an ancient name of Merlin.

Gatto's Keep:
Gatto and Volcanic Trolls

Deep in the realm of the Volcanic Trolls lies Gatto's Keep. Gatto's Keep is a vault that holds many treasures, many of which were locked up by Gatto himself. Gatto is a giant Troll the size of a mountain. Toby and Blinky found the first Triumbric Stone, Gunmar's Birthstone, within it. Also in Gatto's Keep: the Kairosect. This artifact stops time for a maximum of forty-three minutes and nine seconds; however, it can only be used three times and then never again.

Gatto is located underneath Argentina, in a place called Ojos del Salado. Ojos del Salado is a volcano range between Argentina and Chile.

Thankfully, it takes less time to get to Gatto's Keep than you might think traveling by gyre (Trollkind's fastest mode of travel. It goes through sewers and can take you anywhere in the world), but traveling there is not so good for your mobile plan. Roaming fees may apply, so if going to Gatto's Keep, an international smartphone plan is recommended.

Swamps of Quagawumps

Have you ever wondered if there's more to Florida than your grandparents, theme parks, and beaches? Well, there is—Florida is also home to the Quagawumps, a group of Trolls that live deep in the swamps. They are short and stout in nature.

Quagawumps

Quagawumps are typically not friendly to outsiders, especially of the human kind. (On first description, it kind of seems like Quagawumps are similar to alligators, but they're not. At all.)

Quagawumps like to sing and tell stories. They also have a legend of the Shattered King. They believe that one day their king will return. For a while Toby convinced them that he was their king. He can be quite charming.

It was actually pretty easy convincing the Quagawumps that I was their king. They thought my braces were a sign of riches—"a mouth full of precious metals." Ha! Can you believe that? Let's tell the girls at school. . . .

Angor is a deadly villain. Initially, he was a Troll in Bulgaria who used his strength to protect his people. But to increase his power, Angor Rot traded his soul to an evil witch. The witch transferred his soul into a ring called the Inferna Copula.

Angor Rot

The **Inferna Copula** controls Angor Rot. Those who possess the ring, therefore, control this dastardly villain. It was created from Angor Rot's living stone skin.

Angor Rot is armed with a few key things:

Golems: Angor Rot has the magical ability to create giant monsters—Golems—from tiny stone dolls. Remove the carving from the monster's heart, and it dies. Make sure to break the doll so it can't come back.

Shadow Staff: This staff is a magical artifact that can open portals to places you can't even imagine. It can also create darkness so Angor Rot can walk in sunlight. Currently, this staff is in Claire's possession, after taking it from Angor Rot.

Mark of Angor Rot: When I first came face-to-face with Angor Rot, he marked my face with his sigil. This allows him to take the Sword of Daylight from me when my armor is on.

Angor's Eye: Angor Rot can detach his eye from his body, and it acts like a moving camera. Very stealthy. Once placed in the amulet, it also unlocks a new power. It helps the Trollhunter deflect attacks more easily, and it cancels out the mark of Angor.

Creeper's Sun Blade: One of Angor Rot's most deadly weapons is his Creeper's Sun Blade. The blade is laced with a kind of poison that makes good Trolls meet their death by turning them into stone.

Ultimately, after a great battle, this poison would be the thing that killed our poor friend AAARRRGGHH!!!. This causes a great deal of pain to think about.

Strickler, in an attempt to ensure I wouldn't defeat him, summoned Angor Rot to Arcadia Oaks with the Inferna Copula. Angor Rot was after me—and I needed to stop him, as well as Gunmar.

Pixies are extremely small creatures, not to be confused with Fairies. They are like bugs that can fly right into your ear or nose and distort your mind, making you dream your worst nightmare. One day, Angor Rot unleashed them at school to create a diversion to get to me. All the students and teachers went a little nutty . . . including Toby and Claire. I was on

Pixies

my own. Luckily, Toby figured out the cure. Just slap the Pixie out of your head and then use nose- and earplugs so no others can come in again.

PyroBligst

This is a game played in the Hero's Forge. Two teams compete to get the ball, called a gorb, into the Soothscryer. Best out of five wins. Players must earn their weapons, so when I played, I couldn't even use the Amulet at first. It was pretty scary.

Within the deepest caverns underneath Earth's mantle lives a race of Trolls called the Krubera. One note, in case you ever deal with them: the Krubera are large. They are especially sensitive to light because they live their entire lives underground. They were the guardians of the Eye of

The Krubera

Gunmar, but it was stolen by Gumm-Gumms. Because of their close-knit community, they are a bit isolated from the rest of the Trolls, and certainly from Heartstone Trollmarket. Their leader is Queen Usurna. AAARRRGGHH!!! is a Krubera Troll as well. He was taken at a young age to fight in the name of the Gumm-Gumms, but now pledges his allegiance to peace.

We had some (mildly I'll take what I can get) good news come out of Heartstone Trollmarket: Gnome Chompsky had gone to the Darklands some time ago. We'd hoped he could find some information on Claire's brother, Enrique. And he had. He emerged from the Darklands with Enrique's pacifier.

"Enrique!" Claire shouted excitedly. "Is he okay?"

Gnome Chompsky gave a thumbs-up. Then he

removed his hat. His horn was damaged. Gunmar let him escape to give me a message.

I mean, what can you expect from a message from Gunmar? Not good things, you can say.

Gunmar knew I killed his son. And he promised to make a river—an ocean—of blood from my loved ones and make a throne out of my bones. Pretty friendly, huh?

Meanwhile, Angor Rot managed to break into my house . . . while my mom was home. As you might imagine, a lot of things happened all at once.

For one, my mom found out that I was the Trollhunter. She didn't fully understand it, but she understood that there were good Trolls and bad Trolls, and Strickler was somewhere in between.

Speaking of Strickler, he came to my rescue—

somehow. I guess he actually had grown to care for my mom, despite it all.

Strickler noticed that Angor Rot was attacking me, and he promised my mom that he'd help. Strickler told her about magic—though he didn't tell her everything. Poor Mom was probably so overwhelmed that she didn't know what to do.

When Angor was about to finish me, he fell into a trap—set by Strickler and me.

"UV light bulbs. Just like the sun," Strickler said, folding his arms. The sunlight cage kept Angor Rot from escaping.

Just then, my mom raced upstairs and saw Angor Rot.

"Get away from my boy!" she screamed, holding the shovel over her head in midswing.

"Mom, no!" I tried to protest, but she was already set on her plan. My kind, brave mother hit Angor Rot with the shovel. Of course, in doing so, she freed him from the trap.

Next thing I knew, Angor Rot was attacking us in full force. He managed to slash Strickler's neck, which hurt my mom's neck. You see, Strickler had used a Binding Spell on Mom (more on that later), which made anything that happened to one of them, happen to the other.

"Raaaaah!" came an angry voice bursting into the room. It was Draal, slamming into Angor. While Draal pummeled

Angor into the wall, he gave us just enough time to escape.

I needed to cure both Mom and Strickler.

Their wounds wouldn't be healed by modern medicine. I needed to get them to Heartstone Trollmarket.

Strickler got in the driver's seat.

"Are you okay to drive?" I asked.

"Motivated enough, I can do anything," he said.

I held my mom, who was looking weaker and weaker by the second, in the backseat.

"I'm sorry," she said in between gasping breaths.

"No, Mom, I'm sorry," I said. I'd always imagined that I was the one in danger. I never realized that she could have been. "I should have told you. I should have told you everything."

Unfortunately, Strickler was not a very good driver. He was in so much pain, he started to pass out. "Focus!" I said. But then we had something else to worry about: Angor Rot had escaped from Draal's clutches. He was after us.

"We have to shake him!" I yelled. If we entered Heartstone Trollmarket with Angor Rot on our car, it would be a disaster.

Strickler maneuvered the car around in what can only be described as a high-speed chase. I yelled out instructions for how to get to Heartstone Trollmarket, while Toby, whom I'd called, worked on getting the Horngazel just right.

"Come on, Tobes, come on," I said desperately, hoping my friend was able to do it.

And then—*boom.* The Horngazel worked. Angor Rot was off our vehicle. We dove right into Heartstone Trollmarket—me and Mom and Strickler.

"We need help," I said when we arrived, hoisting my mom up. "Please."

Binding Spell

As I've mentioned, some time ago, Strickler used a Binding Spell to bind himself to my mom. With the Binding Spell, anything that happened to one, happened to the other. This ensured I'd never kill Strickler, or else I'd kill my mom, too.

Over time, however, Strickler developed real feelings for my mom. When Angor Rot hurt her, he wanted to help. After I promised to let him go free, he told us the Unbinding Spell was located in *The Book of Ga-huel* in his office at school. Toby and Claire snuck in and got it.

"Quickly, bring them both inside the examination dwell," Vendel said.

"Only the Fates can know what will happen," Blinky said. "Barbara's only hope is to break the spell that entwines her fate with Strickler's. If Vendel can do that, maybe she'll be strong enough to survive on her own."

While Vendel worked on my mom and Strickler, I paced outside the room. I couldn't believe it. It was all my fault. I kept thinking "if only, if only, if only." All I wanted was my mom to be safe. I'd do anything for that.

Finally, Vendel came out of the examination dwell. I was allowed to go visit her.

When I saw her, I breathed a sigh of relief. Mom was still in critical danger, but at least now she looked like herself. She had a lot of questions.

"So, when you and your friends said you were going camping, you were . . . ," she started.

"We were getting a Triumbric Stone from a place called Gatto's Keep," I said. (I conveniently left out that this was in Argentina.)

"It's just too much," Mom said weakly.

"I should have told you sooner," I said. "Maybe none of this would have ever happened."

Vendel joined us now. "Breaking the Binding Spell will also erase her memory," he told me.

My mom looked up. "What are you saying? I'm going to forget Trollmarket? That Jim's the Trollhunter?"

"Guess we're going to have this conversation again," I laughed, trying to lighten the mood. I wanted to have the conversation again more than anything. Because that would mean there was an "again."

"Promise me we will," said Mom. "It took all this for you to tell me about your other life. But listen to me—I want you to know something. Even before you found this Amulet, way before all this, you were always my hero, my beautiful boy."

I held on to her hand tight.

"I love you, Mom," I said.

Once my mom was safe, I
hopped on my Vespa and met up
with Claire. We may have missed
most of Spring Fling, and Steve
Palchuck may have been named

king (oh yeah, I'd forgotten I was in the running—maybe
missing all of those Fling King campaigns hadn't exactly
helped), but it was time for us to go on a date. On a real
date. You know? Like normal teenagers. Who battle Trolls.

I know this isn't exactly about Trollhunting, but
remember what Strickler said, back before he knew I
was the Trollhunter? "Do what's good for you or you're
not good for anybody." Going on a date with Claire was
good for me. And sometimes, you just have to do that.

Claire put on her helmet, and we rode over to a cliff at
the edge of town. It was no Spring Fling, but I figured we
could have our own little dance, of sorts. Something that wasn't
dangerous. Something that wouldn't get us killed by monsters.

Claire and I danced together under the moonlight,
surrounded by soft music. It was more magical than any
Spring Fling could have possibly been. Everything was
smooth sailing . . . until Claire started looking panicked.

"No, no, no, no!" she said.

"What? Is it my breath?" I asked. Of course, in my

haste, I hadn't checked to see if my breath was okay!

"No! He has it! He has it!" Claire screeched. She was frenzied.

Then Claire explained: while getting the incantation for my mom at school, she and Toby had run into Angor Rot. Angor Rot stole her purse. She hadn't realized it at the time, but in her purse . . . was a Horngazel, the key to Heartstone Trollmarket.

Oh, dear reader. I'm afraid I have some dreadful news. Something terrible has happened. I have taken over the journal and made some notes in these pages.

I do hope this documented "manual," as Master Jim so often called it, serves you well.

As it happens, the Changeling by the name of Mr. Strickler truly did care for Jim's mother. He gave our Jim the final Triumbric Stone—the Eye of Gunmar—that he'd been holding on to for generations. With the three stones in place, Jim was ready to defeat Angor Rot—and kill Gunmar.

Master Jim donned the Trollhunter armor and raced to Heartstone Trollmarket, where Angor Rot had entered and was causing mass panic. Master Jim held his own in battle and wielded his sword well . . . but it was a terrible fight.

Unfortunately, in battle, AAARRRGGHH!!! sacrificed

himself to our plight. He jumped in front of a dagger that would have brought certain death upon young Tobias.

AAARRRGGHH!!! and Tobias had just enough time to lock hands before AAARRRGGHH!!! was turned to stone completely. AAARRRGGHH!!! died valiantly, and

one could not ask for a more honorable way to go than by sacrificing yourself for a friend.

Enraged by AAARRRGGHH!!!'s demise, young Tobias was the one to deal the final blow to Angor Rot's stone body, after Jim had poisoned him with his own Creeper's Sun Blade. He brought much honor upon himself—and upon AAARRRGGHH!!!'s name. The Trollhunters who lost their lives to Angor Rot were held within him and returned to the Ghost Forge, to live their deaths in peace.

The spirit of the great Trollhunter Kanjigar the Courageous came to deliver this news himself. But he gave Master Jim a warning, too.

"The day will come, Trollhunter, when you must finish the fight alone," he said.

Unfortunately, that gave Master Jim an idea. He did not want to see any more of his friends hurt. He hurried to Killahead Bridge himself . . . alone.

"For the doom of Gunmar, Eclipse is mine to command!"

Master Jim said boldly, transforming his Trollhunter armor and Amulet into that of the Eclipse. He had done what no Trollhunter had done before: he had cobbled together the Triumbric Stones to stand a chance against Gunmar's defeat.

I tried to stop him. I really did. "Master Jim!" I called.

"You promised we'd go together!" Claire yelled.

But despite all of our warnings, Master Jim had made up his mind.

"The Amulet chose me. I can't lose any more of you," he said. "I'm sorry."

And then he left, descending downward into the Darklands.

Master Jim, if you ever read this—
what have you done?
Will you ever return?

This is why, as you can see, we need you now more than ever. Master Jim has descended into the Darklands, and we need as many Trollhunters as we can get. Are you ready to join the ranks of Trollhunters? Master Jim could not answer all these questions when he began, but perhaps you will be able to. Test your skills in Trollhunting with the questions below. As they say in Heartstone Trollmarket, may the daylight be with you!

1.   Who wrote *A Brief Recapitulation of Troll Lore*?
    a.   Blinky
    b.   Deya the Deliverer
    c.   Kanjigar the Courageous
    d.   The Venerable Bedehilde

2.   When it comes to Gnomes, what is one thing you should never, ever do?
    ever do?
    a.   Speak German to them
    b.   Touch their hats
    c.   Take care of them
    d.   Cook tacos with them

3. What is the correct incantation to activate the Amulet of Daylight?
   a. "For the glory of Merlin, Daylight is mine to command."
   b. "For the vengeance of Morgana, Daylight is mine to command."
   c. "For the love of pizza, Daylight is mine to command."
   d. "For the terror of goblins, moonlight is mine to command."

4. Which of the following is NOT a rule of Trollhunting?
   a. Always finish the fight.
   b. Always be afraid.
   c. Kick them in the gronk-nuks.
   d. The Trollhunter buys everyone pizza.

5. Which of the following is NOT a kind of Troll?
   a. Krubera
   b. Volcanic
   c. Cheesy
   d. Gumm-Gumm

6. What is the name of the ring that controls Angor Rot?
   a. Inferna Copula
   b. Angor Rot's Ring
   c. Exitio Circulum
   d. Caseus Trollem

7. What tool is used to discover who is a Changeling?

   a. Gaggletack
   b. Giggletoe
   c. Changeling Stone
   d. Really Old Bread

8. Which of the following is NOT a part of Heartstone Trollmarket?

   a. Crystal Stairs
   b. Bagdwella's Fine Gifts
   c. Angor Rot's Apothecary
   d. Troll Pub

9. Which of the following Trolls was a former general in Gunmar's army?

   a. AAARRRGGHH!!!
   b. Bular
   c. Kanjigar the Courageous
   d. Sir Pizza Rolls

10. What can a Trollhunter not refuse?

   a. Pizza
   b. Pizza Rolls
   c. Stuffed Pizza Crust
   d. The call

G

H

I

P

Q

R

X

Y

Z

8

9

0

ALPHABET

D

E

F

M

N

O

U

V

W

4

5

6

7